ONCE UPON
A STORMY NIGHT

a Stormy Night
© 2016 by Katelin Sullivan. All rights reserved.

his publication may be reproduced, stored in a retrieval system or transmitted by any means, electronic, mechanical, photocopy, recording or otherwise prior permission of the author except as provided by USA copyright law.

taken from the *Holy Bible, New International Version®*, NIV®. Copyright 78, 1984 by Biblica, Inc.™ Used by permission of Zondervan. All rights rldwide. www.zondervan.com

is a work of fiction. Names, descriptions, entities, and incidents included in e products of the author's imagination. Any resemblance to actual persons, entities is entirely coincidental.

ns expressed by the author are not necessarily those of Tate Publishing,

y Tate Publishing & Enterprises, LLC
le Center Terrace | Mustang, Oklahoma 73064 USA
473 | www.tatepublishing.com

hing is committed to excellence in the publishing industry. The company philosophy established by the founders, based on Psalm 68:11,
gave the word and great was the company of those who published it."

n copyright © 2016 by Tate Publishing, LLC. All rights reserved.
 by *Joana Quilantang*
gn by *Shieldon Alcasid*

the United States of America

1-68301-302-0
Christian / General
Christian Life / General

KATELIN SU

ON(

A STORMY

TATE PUBLIS
AND ENTERPRISE

To Heather Metzger

The Lord is my light and my salvation—whom shall I fear? The Lord is the stronghold of my life—of whom shall I be afraid?

—Psalm 27:1

God bless you and keep you always.

For I was hungry and you gave me something to eat, I was thirsty and you gave me something to drink, I was a stranger and you invited me in, I needed clothes and you clothed me, I was sick and you looked after me, I was in prison and you came to visit me.

Truly I tell you, whatever you did for one of the least of these brothers of mine, you did for me.

—Matthew 25:35–36, 40 (NIV)

Heeter McLaughlin hopped from one foot to the other with a toothy grin on his freckled face. His eyes gleamed mischievously. He suspended a green ribbon in the air with his fingers.

Metta, his sister, held the ribbon's match.

"Give it back," Metta fumed, glowering. She closed the distance between herself and her brother by taking one long stride.

Heeter, grinning ridiculously, bolted. His stringy blond hair flew out behind him.

Gathering up a fistful of her dress, Metta raced after Heeter. She cleared the fence in a spectacular jump but landed in a puddle of mud on the ground. Embarrassed, Metta picked herself up, straightening her muddied skirts. Resuming the chase with less reckless abandon than before, she dodged around the clothesline and sprinted toward the house.

A big wooden sign, all painted up with the words McLaughlin Trading Post, passed its shadow over Metta as she ran underneath it. It creaked back and forth, hanging from the porch by a couple of metal hooks.

"It ain't much to show for eight weeks, but the weather has put a hold on most of the trapping this year. First, it was the snow, then the rain. How much salt do you have? I'll be needin' at least half of it."

Since the man's back was facing her, all Metta saw were broad shoulders, a dirty overcoat, and oily red hair glistening on the back of his head. An impressive accumulation of furs were scattered around his massive boots. He was standing at the counter, talking to Mr. McLaughlin, her father.

Out of the corner of her eye, Metta saw a flash of green and blue.

Heeter.

She was back on the trail again.

"I think all our bad weather is headed your way, McLaughlin," the man predicted, hauling up an armload of furs onto the counter. "The darkest storm clouds I've ever seen followed me all the way here from Shuckstack falls. You can guarantee it; it'll be raining down on this place like cats and dogs in no time."

Moving carefully, Metta zigzagged around barrels and sacks of coffee, sugar, flour, and salt. She snaked through stacks and bolts of cloth, hides, and tarps. Metta stepped over boxes and cases of nails, hammers, saws, and axes.

And then she tripped over a broom.

Mr. McLaughlin looked up. "Watch your step, Metta," he chided.

Metta put the broom upright and leaned it against the wall. Then she heard someone snickering.

And she knew who it was.

With the agility of a cat, Metta sprang over the pots and kettles and crouched down in front of a mountain of woolen blankets. She ripped the top blanket off.

Heeter sat there, laughing at her.

"Give me my ribbon," demanded Metta, her voice low and tight.

"Not until you say, 'Little Bo Peep has lost her sheep and doesn't know where to find them.' Say it." Heeter grinned, his buckteeth sticking out.

"No," Metta refused. "That's silly."

"Then no ribbon."

Metta glared at him. Crossing her arms, she quickly repeated, "Little Bo Peep has lost her sheep and doesn't know where to find them." She stretched out her hand. "Give me my ribbon—now."

Heeter chortled. "I don't have it. I lost it outside when I was running to the house." He wrinkled his nose. "You're like little Bo Peep—only you've lost your ribbon instead of your sheep."

She couldn't believe it. "You are teeerible!" Metta lunged for him, but Heeter shot out from under the woolen blankets like greased lightning, and Metta crashed into an empty pile of bedspreads. Outraged, she lay there for a moment, trying to get a hold on her temper.

"You're not in a very ladylike position. I can see you haven't changed in the slightest. Goodness, Metta. Straighten your hair and fix your skirt. You're embarrassing me." Metta grimaced at the shrill feminine voice that addressed her.

This day was becoming a nightmare.

Detangling herself from the layers of hot and stiff blankets proved to be more difficult than Metta had expected. But, when she finally got into a sitting position, Metta stared up at a most unwelcome visitor.

Elsa.

Her dress was completely covered with ruffles, bows, lace, ribbons, and curls, and she was full of prissiness. Her nose tilted up, and her eyes looked down disapprovingly at Metta.

"Aren't you going to stand up?" Elsa prodded, raising her hands.

Heeter grinned. "I think she'd rather stay on the floor. The view is better down there."

"Stay out of this, Heeter!" Metta jumped to her feet. "I'm standing, aren't I?"

Elsa raised an eyebrow. "Don't talk like that to Heeter," she reprimanded. "It's not like it was his fault that you are all spread out in a messy heap on the ground."

"It *was* his fault!" Metta shouted.

"Don't shout, Metta," Mr. McLaughlin lectured.

Metta blushed in embarrassment.

"Elsa is staying here for a little while," Heeter informed, grinning outrageously at Elsa. For reasons beyond Metta's comprehension, Heeter seemed impressed with Elsa's ruffles, bows, lace, ribbons, curls, and prissiness.

His infatuation disgusted Metta.

"Why?" Metta demanded for an answer. "And how long is a 'little while'?"

"Goodness, Metta," Elsa exclaimed, pretending to look upset. "You sound like you can't wait for me to go."

"I can't." Metta answered honestly.

"You'll be good, won't you, Elsa?" When the man with the broad shoulders, dirty overcoat, and oily red hair turned around, Metta recognized him as Elsa's father, Mr. Ramsey. His enormous boots thudded over to them, and he leaned forward.

"Of course I will, Father," Elsa promised, her silky voice gliding through the air like a slippery snake. She caught Metta's scrutinizing glance and added, "It will all be quite marvelous; Metta and I are the best of friends."

Metta couldn't believe that Elsa lied to her father.

Before Metta had a chance to contradict Elsa's false statement, Mr. Ramsey had exchanged a quick good-bye and was gone.

"It's startin' to rain," Noah McLaughlin announced, tromping through the front door and shaking out his coat vigorously. He noticed Elsa, and his eyes sparked. "Hello, Miss Elsa." He tipped his hat.

Elsa smiled charmingly.

Metta couldn't believe that her brother had fallen for Elsa's ruffles, bows, lace, ribbons, curls, and her prissiness as well. She crossed her arms with a huff.

Reed, the oldest McLaughlin sibling, shut the door after his brother. He slipped his arms out of his wet coat and leaned over to Metta's shoulder, whispering, "Noah's in love."

Metta rolled her eyes. "That's ridiculous. And what do you know about love anyway?"

Heeter ran to the window and pressed his face against the glass, watching with fascination as raindrops began to fall harder and faster against the dry ground.

"I hate getting wet." Elsa puckered her lips distastefully.

"Then I'd better get you a bucket," Metta mused out loud, her lips curving into a wry smile.

Elsa glared. "Why would I need a stupid bucket?"

"Because the roof leaks."

"It's leaking over here!" Heeter wailed, throwing his hands up in the air. "And we don't have any more pans!" He cupped his hands to catch the rain.

Metta stared at a single raindrop as it slid down from the ceiling and plopped into the stew that sat on the stove. All of a sudden, the rain came pouring down hard and fast. She picked up the pot and carried it over to the table.

Boom!

Metta jumped at the sudden loud crash of thunder, and the pot hit the table with a loud bang. She recovered quickly, pretending that the thunder hadn't bothered her so much.

But Heeter saw and laughed.

"Don't laugh!" Metta howled.

"I ain't laughin'," Heeter said. "I'm merely smiling out loud." He grinned outrageously, thinking of himself as terribly clever.

Metta scowled at him.

The back room of the trading post was where the McLaughlin family lived. It was awfully small, little beds were stuffed into corners and big beds were shoved against the wall, an old woodstove was jammed next to the door, and a nice round table was right in the middle of the room. It was all very cramped, tight, and overcrowded.

But with Elsa there, it seemed even more so.

Elsa sat prissily on a little stool right by the table. Her legs were crossed, and her gloved hands were folded in her lap. She observed the comings and goings of the McLaughlin family both primly and critically. She was, in short, doing nothing and proving herself to be more of a hindrance than a help.

The chair legs scraped against the wooden floor as Mr. McLaughlin dragged a seat next to his wife's bed. He sat down, saying, "Metta and Elsa, set the table. Noah and Reed, come help me move your mother's bed. The roof's starting to leak on the blankets."

Reed and Noah marched over to the bed, crouched down, and simultaneously lifted it from the ground. Metta watched as her older brothers carried it a few feet and then gently laid the bed down due to its delicate passenger.

Metta turned around, grabbed a stack of bowls, and bumped into Elsa.

"What's wrong with her?" Elsa asked, gawking at Metta's mother who was all wrapped up in blankets and covers and looking more sick and weak than ever.

Metta swallowed hard. "She's sick."

"Metta, get another blanket for your mother," said Mr. McLaughlin, tucking in the blankets around his wife's shoulders and feet. He then held her hand.

Wiping her nose, Metta went over to the trunk that was pushed up against Reed's bed and lifted the big, heavy lid. She rummaged around for a thick quilt and pulled out a bright yellow one. Yellow was her mother's favorite color. The wooden lid of the trunk creaked as she shut it.

"Thank you, Metta," her mother said, smiling softly as Metta handed her the quilt. Her eyes were tired, and her body was worn down from fighting a sickness that Metta didn't understand and her father couldn't cure.

And even though she didn't feel like it, Metta smiled back.

"When are we eating?" Heeter jumped up and down and waved his arms.

"Stop jumping," Metta scolded. "We're eating now." She ladled out seven bowls—three big bowls for her father, Reed, and Noah; three medium bowls for Heeter, Elsa, and herself; and one small bowl for her mother.

Reed started praying, "Thank you, Jesus, for the food we eat. Please don't let the rain cause too much damage and help everyone who might be out in the weather find warm shelter tonight. Also, Lord Jesus, heal my Ma. In Jesus's name. Amen."

Metta raised her head and huddled over by the fire, folding her knees up against her chest. It had suddenly become very cold, both outside and indoors. Shoveling her spoon into the stew, she started eating as she watched the rain beat mercilessly against the glass windows.

Heeter crawled up on his bed, burrowed under his blankets, and started eating his supper. He listened to the thunder rumble, crash, and boom.

Reed and Noah pulled their chairs as close to the stove as they could get. And even though the wind was blowing furiously and the thunder was crashing violently, they didn't look up until they had eaten all their stew.

Elsa picked at her food, sighing. "When is it going to stop raining?"

"I don't know." Reed scraped the last bit of supper out of his bowl and looked up at the window. "It may last all night. Hopefully, it doesn't flood Bear Creek."

"I'm tired of the rain." Elsa wrapped her arms around her shoulders and rocked back and forth on the stool. "I hate getting wet," she muttered irritably as rain fell from the ceiling and splashed into the buckets that were placed all around the room.

Noah looked at Elsa with stars in his eyes as he vowed solemnly, "I won't let you get wet, Elsa. I promise."

At that moment, a big, wet raindrop fell on top of Elsa's head. Her lower lip stuck out in an enormous pout.

Heeter horselaughed.

Metta rolled her eyes.

Noah looked stricken.

And Reed said, "Don't make promises you can't keep, old Romeo." He grinned and pushed Noah off his chair and onto the floor.

"God is our refuge and strength, an ever-present help in trouble. Therefore, we will not fear, though the earth gives away and the mountains fall into the heart of the sea, though its waters roar and foam and the mountains quake with their surging…"

Noah looked up from the floor. Metta cupped her chin in her hands.

Their father was reading the Bible to their mother.

"There is a river whose streams make glad the city of God, the holy place where the Most High dwells. God is within her, she will not fall; God will help her at the break of day…"

Heeter stopped laughing. Reed helped Noah off the floor.

"Nations are in uproar, kingdoms fall; he lifts his voice, the earth melts. The Lord Almighty is with us; the God of Jacob is our fortress…"

Their father's voice was so strong, calm, and clear.

And their mother, though tired and worn-out, looked peaceful.

"Come and see the works of the Lord—the desolations he has brought on the earth. He makes wars cease to the ends of the earth; he breaks the bow and shatters the spear, he burns the shields with fire. Be still and know that I am God; I will be exalted among the nations, I will be exalted in the earth…"

Elsa looked like she had never heard anything like that before, and Metta figured that she hadn't.

"The Lord Almighty is with us; the God of Jacob—"
Knock, knock!
Everyone looked up at the door.
Knock, knock, knock!
"Get the door, Noah," their father said.
Knock, knock, knock, knock!
Noah opened the door, and the wind banged it against the wall.

A man with a big belly and a little short mustache poked his head inside the house. Drenched from head to foot, he looked around at everyone crowded in the little room and asked Noah, "Is this the Charles Bunion Hotel?"

"No, sir. This is the McLaughlin Trading Post." Noah answered and then said, "But you can come in anyway." He stepped away from the door, giving the man some room to come inside.

"Thank you." The man expressed his appreciation as he shuffled in and shook the rain out of his overcoat. A large puddle formed at his feet. Then, leaning his head out the door, he spoke to someone outside, saying, "It's all right, Bertha dear. Bring the children inside."

Mrs. Bertha Plinkerton held a huge umbrella over her head. She was short, stout, and plump. A chubby little girl with bright blond hair peered out shyly from behind her skirt, and she carried another little girl on her hip. Three stout little boys paraded behind her. Bertha, all very wet and tired, looked up at her husband, "Is this the Charles Bunion Hotel, Heinrich dear?"

"No, Bertha dear," her husband, Mr. Heinrich Plinkerton, replied. "This is the McLaughlin Trading Post. But they let us in anyway—quite obliging of them."

Metta got up, took their wet coats, and hung them up to dry by the stove.

"I'm sorry to take advantage of your hospitality, being a perfect stranger to you all," Heinrich told Mr. McLaughlin. "But if you would be kind enough to give us a moment to recover our strength and dry out a bit, we'll move on as soon as possible."

Mr. McLaughlin shook his head. "On a night like this, I wouldn't turn anybody out."

Mrs. Plinkerton, bedraggled, looked like she was about to cry. "Thank you so much."

Elsa poked Metta in the side and whispered, "Your dad better not mean that because if this keeps up, there won't be any room."

Metta stared at Elsa. "Maybe we'll turn you out in this storm."

Elsa didn't say anything else.

"Warm up the stew again, Metta," Mrs. McLaughlin tried to sit up but fell back weakly. "They're all probably starving."

Heeter jumped off his bed and leaned over Metta's shoulder as she put a piece of wood in the stove and stirred the stew. "Give me some more stew too, Metta." He hopped on one foot and then hopped on the other. "I'm hungrier than anybody here."

Metta slapped his hand away when he tried to put his finger in the stew. "I'm not getting you anymore; you've already had plenty. Besides," she confided. "there isn't very much stew left."

"You're the worst sister I've got." Heeter stuck out his tongue.

"I'm your only sister," Metta said dryly.

Heeter scrunched up his eyebrows. "What's that got to do with anything?" He scrambled away and jumped up on his bed and lay there.

"We're taking up room in your house." Bertha watched Metta heat up supper and bring it to the table. "We don't need to eat your food too." She opened the knapsack that they had been carrying and pulled out a couple of soggy loaves of bread and three cans of sauerkraut. "You shouldn't give your food to strangers."

"Ma'am," Mr. McLaughlin drawled, "we're all strangers here."

It took a few minutes, but Metta managed to find some extra bowls and dished out the food to the Plinkerton family. The girls, Gretel and Birgit, sat at the table with their parents while they ate, but the three little boys, Wolfie, Günter, and Stefan, climbed up on Heeter's bed. Stefan accidently spilled some of the stew on Heeter's pillow. Metta thought it was funny, but Heeter wasn't very happy.

"As Jesus was on his way, the crowds almost crushed him. And a woman was there who had been subject to bleeding for twelve years, but no one could heal her. She came up behind him and touched the edge of his cloak, and immediately, her bleeding stopped."

Metta looked up. It was her mother's favorite Bible story.

"'Who touched me?' Jesus asked. When they all denied it, Peter said, 'Master, the people are crowding and pressing against you.' But Jesus said, 'Someone touched me; I know that power has gone out from me.'"

Mrs. McLaughlin gazed intently at her husband, watching every word come off his lips. Her face shone with hope.

"Then the woman, seeing that she could not go unnoticed, came trembling and fell at his feet. In the presence of all the people, she told why she had touched him and how she had been instantly healed. Then he said to her, 'Daughter, your faith has healed you. Go in peace.'"

Mama sucked in a deep breath full of faith and anticipation.

Metta realized why her mother loved that part of the Bible so much.

Mama wanted to be healed by Jesus too.

Knock, knock!

"Why can't people go someplace else?" Elsa grumbled under her breath.

This time, Reed got up and opened the door.

"Looks like you've already got company, McLaughlin." Old George leaned in the door, his battered hat pulled down over his wrinkled face. "I didn't know if you folks would still be awake, but I saw the light in the window and came in to ask for a place to get out of the weather. My passengers are wet as drowned rats; the storm came up quicker than I expected. Do you have any room?"

"You got the stagecoach with you?" Reed raised his eyebrows. "Couldn't you make it to town?"

"That stagecoach is pulled right up to your porch step and unless you folks got a couple paddles that I can borrow, it ain't going one inch further," Old George said grimly.

"We got plenty of room," Mr. McLaughlin said firmly. "Reed, let Old George come in and you and Noah go out and help bring the passengers inside. Stable the horses in the barn. Make it quick."

Noah and Reed jumped into their boots and dashed outside in the rain. Old George hobbled over to the stove and tried to warm up. At first, Old George didn't see Mrs. McLaughlin in the bed, but when he did, he started.

"Mrs. McLaughlin." Old George doffed his hat and tramped over to her bedside. "Are you taken with a cold?" He flipped his hand toward the door. "I've got two passengers that are bound to have a whale of a cold tomorrow."

Mr. McLaughlin's eyes were grim. "I'm afraid it's a bit more serious than that, George."

Old George's face screwed up, and he wiped his nose. "I'm real sorry, Emma." He looked like his heart had broken. "I really am."

Reed and Noah carried an unconscious young man through the door. A red bloodstain spread across the upper part of his shirt.

"Who robbed you?" Heeter shouted, dashing over and staring at the wounded man. "Was it anybody famous? Tel Murphy? Lexie Stone's boys? Or even Billy the Kid?"

Old George squashed his hat back up on his head. "Ain't nobody robbed nobody." He helped the two boys lower the young man down onto Reed's bed. "This young feller was riding shotgun for me, and when he was cleaning his gun, he accidently shot himself."

Heeter looked at the young man disappointedly. "That wasn't very smart."

Noah and Reed ran back outside, and Old George stared at the young man with uncertainty. "I don't know how to go about getting that bullet out properly. I'd do more damage than good, I reckon."

Mr. Plinkerton pushed back his chair and grabbed a few medical instruments out of their bag. He opened the top of the young man's shirt and examined the wound. He looked at Metta. "Go get your mama's biggest kettle and fill it with water. Bring it to a boil."

"What's his name?" Elsa studied the young man with interest as he lay unconscious.

"Creaky Joe," Old George answered. "At least, that's what he goes by."

"Is there anybody else?" Heeter pushed his head out the door into the rain.

Reed brought in five more muddy passengers. They stood, dripping in the doorway, at a loss of what to do with themselves. Quickly, Reed snatched a couple of towels and passed them around. When they had cleaned themselves up the best they could, Metta distinguished an elderly woman, a middle-aged man and his wife and son, and a teenage girl.

"Pull out those boxes so that we have more seats, Reed," Mr. McLaughlin instructed, rising up, and offering his own seat to the elderly woman. The woman sat down with relief.

Metta checked the kettle. The water was just about to boil.

"Can I help?" The teenage girl had pulled her hair down, and it hung damp across her shoulders and down her back. Her face was kind. She was a couple of years older than Metta. With a sweet smile, she introduced herself, "I'm Claire by the way." She nodded toward the elderly woman who had taken Mr. McLaughlin's seat. "That's Naomi, she's my great-aunt."

"I'm Metta. Mr. Plinkerton needs this water for Creaky Joe," Metta explained. "He's going to take the bullet out."

Claire took the fireplace poker off the hook and stoked the fire. "Is there anything you need me to help you move?" Glancing around, Claire continued, "It's going to get a little crowded in here."

"It already is crowded." Elsa walked up, scowling. She gave Metta a look. "I wish I wasn't here."

"I'm glad I'm here," Claire said gratefully. "The storm out there is terrible."

Creaky Joe let out a groan, twisting and turning on the bed. Mr. Plinkerton held him still. "The water, Metta—is it ready?"

"Yes, sir."

Together, Metta and Claire hauled the water over to Mr. Plinkerton. He dipped his instruments in it slowly and laid them neatly on the trunk in front of the bed. "McLaughlin." He looked up at Mr. McLaughlin a second. "Do you have any extra sheets I can rip into bandages?"

"Heeter, get whatever Heinrich needs," Daddy instructed.

During the next hour, Metta boiled more water, rearranged the bunks with Claire, washed the dishes, corralled the five Plinkerton children, made her mother and Aunt Naomi some tea, cleaned up all the muddy footprints on the floor and dumped buckets of water—all the while trying to avoid running into somebody every time she turned around.

Elsa sat around and didn't offer any help.

Metta almost tripped over Reed's legs as she carried an armload of dirty towels to the hamper basket. His eyes were alight with fascination. He didn't even seem to mind that she had nearly fallen on top of him.

She scrutinized him for a minute and then asked, "What are you looking at?"

Reed murmured as if he was in a dream, "I ain't seen anybody like her."

Metta followed his gaze, and it went all the way across the room to Claire.

Claire, with a Plinkerton baby nearly asleep on her hip, was bringing more tea to Aunt Naomi. Her face aglow with kindness and compassion as she brought more bandages to Mr. Plinkerton. She also laid a pillow against Old George's chair to help relieve his bad back.

"I've seen plenty of pretty girls," Reed wouldn't peel his eyes off of Claire. "But not one of them was as half as kind as her."

Heeter jumped up, his buckteeth shining as he sang. "Reed and Claire, sitting on a tree—"

Reed clamped his hand over Heeter's mouth.

Heeter let out a muffled guffaw.

Old George twisted his hat in his hands awkwardly, looking at Mr. McLaughlin with his shy but honest face. He cleared his throat, saying, "All of us are mighty grateful to you folks for letting us stay here till the storm dies down. I owe you a lot, and I ain't but got a few pennies in my pocket. So," Old George tried to stand up erect and straighten the hump in his back. "I was wondering if I could offer you my prayers—for the missus there."

Mr. McLaughlin reached out for his wife's hand. When he found it, he swallowed hard. "We'd appreciate it, George."

Old George fumbled for Mrs. McLaughlin's other hand, and she took it. Her hand looked so white and pale, and his was so tan and weathered. And then Old George stretched out his fingers, searching for Metta's hand.

She wrapped her small fingers around his, and he grasped it firmly. Metta groped for Noah, and he reached out to Heeter who grabbed onto Reed, and somehow, Claire ended up being right there and linked her fingers with his. Claire hooked arms with Naomi. Mrs. Plinkerton stood in between three of the other passengers, and they formed a circle with their hands adjoined all around Mrs. McLaughlin's bed.

Elsa just sat there and looked.

"Girl," Old George noticed her. "I don't know your name, but how about you come on over here and stand with us? Mrs. McLaughlin needs Jesus to heal her."

Metta could tell that Elsa didn't want to stand up and come over, but for some reason, she did anyway. Noah broke apart from Metta, and Elsa reluctantly stepped between the two of them.

Metta reached out for Elsa.

But Elsa wouldn't take her hand.

"Lord, Mrs. McLaughlin here is feeling sick in a bad way, and there ain't nothing any one of us standing here can do about it. But I know as sure as anything that You're able to do whatever You set Your mind to doing," Old George prayed, his gravelly voice speaking out in the hushed room. "And ain't nothing too hard for You to get done. So if You see that it's fitting, heal the missus here and make her well and healthy again." He coughed a little, his voice cracking. "'Cause I ain't met nobody around these parts that can cook or sing Your praises like Emma McLaughlin, Lord." Old George choked up a little, and it took him a minute before he went on, "These McLaughlin young'uns need their Mama, so give her strength so she can stay around and be one to them."

Metta sniffled.

"Help Creaky Joe over there pull through and keep all of us safe tonight in this bad weather," Old George cleared his throat again. "We know we can trust You no matter what. In Jesus's name. Amen."

Everyone said amen.

Before anyone noticed, Metta wiped her eyes with the back of her sleeve. She glanced over at Old George for a second. He was looking at Mrs. McLaughlin, tears making tracks down his cheeks. Metta was no longer ashamed of her tears, and she stopped drying her eyes.

"Thank you, George," Mrs. McLaughlin said softly.

Old George crushed his hat back on top of his head and said, "You're going to get well, Mrs. McLaughlin. Jesus will heal you."

Mrs. McLaughlin smiled. "I know."

"I got the bullet out," Mr. Plinkerton announced, scrubbing his hands in warm water and then drying them on one of the less dirty towels. The bullet clinked as he dropped it down into a metal cup.

Heeter dashed over and snatched up the bullet. "Can I keep it?" He held it high, staring at it in the lamplight.

Mr. Plinkerton shrugged toward Creaky Joe. "I don't think he'll be wanting it around anymore, but when he wakes up, you'll have to ask him."

Creaky Joe stirred groggily.

Shoving the bullet in Creaky Joe's face, Heeter shouted, "Can I keep your bullet?"

"You got it out," Creaky Joe murmured, gazing up at Mr. Plinkerton with relief. "I guess my luck seems to be running pretty good."

"It didn't have anything to do with your luck, son." Mr. Plinkerton gathered up his medical equipment and started to walk away. He looked back. "God just saw fit to save you. If that bullet had been a couple fractions to the left, you wouldn't be around anymore."

Creaky Joe was suddenly quiet.

"Nobody is here on this earth by accident," Mr. Plinkerton said. "And I'm not in this house tonight by accident and neither are you. God knew that you'd be needing someone to take that bullet out, and God knew that I could." He looked at Creaky Joe for a long time. "Not a sparrow falls to the ground apart from the Lord's will." He shoved his medical tools back into his bag. "And because of God's love for you, you didn't either."

"Thank you," Creaky Joe whispered, his lips trembling.

Mr. Plinkerton nodded with understanding.

"Where am I going to sleep?" Heeter bounded across the room. Opening and closing his hand, he gazed at the bullet with some sort of awe. He stuck his finger out, pointing. "Wolfie, Günter, and Stefan stole my bed."

Metta shot a quick glance. Heeter was right. The three Plinkerton boys were sound asleep on his bunk. "I don't know where anybody is going to sleep," Metta groused, throwing Heeter a blanket and pillow. "You might have to sleep standing up."

Heeter shut one eye and glared at her with the other. "How does someone go to sleep standing up?"

he demanded. "Don't your legs get tired from standing all night?"

"Try it and find out," Metta challenged, smirking.

Heeter stuck out his tongue.

There was a half an hour of disorganized chaos as sleeping arrangements were made. Nearly everybody wanted to sleep on a bed, but there weren't enough beds to go around. As it all ended up, Creaky Joe was privileged to get a bunk because nobody wanted to move him for fear that he would start bleeding again. Mr. and Mrs. Plinkerton took over Reed and Noah's bed while the boys camped out on the floor by the stove. Heeter managed to squeeze in between the three chubby Plinkerton boys, and Old George pushed two of the chairs together for a makeshift cot. Claire shared Metta's bed with her elderly aunt.

Elsa and Metta lay down on the floor at the foot of Mr. and Mrs. McLaughlin's bed.

Metta looked around, watching Mr. McLaughlin blow out the lamps. Creaky Joe was already sound asleep. Old George, his scruffy hat tugged down over his eyes, was snoring loudly. Heeter kept tossing and turning uncomfortably in his bed with the three Plinkerton boys.

"I don't like to sleep on the floor," Elsa grumbled from under the blankets. "It's hard and cold and dirty." She rolled up in a tight ball, pulling all the blankets around her. "I wish I was with Daddy." Her voice was hardly above a whisper, but Metta heard her anyway.

And all of a sudden, Metta felt sorry for her.

"He'll be back before you know it," Metta encouraged, whispering softly under the blankets.

Elsa snorted. "Yeah, and won't that make you happy?" She rolled on her side, her back to Metta.

Metta swallowed, shamefaced.

Noah chucked his shoe in Metta's direction. It nearly hit her head. "Metta, be quiet and go to sleep." He griped sleepily.

"*You* go to sleep." Metta picked up the stinky boot and tossed it back.

It hit Reed with a loud thud.

"Sorry," Metta apologized quickly.

It didn't take long before everyone was asleep. Old George and Mr. Plinkerton were snoring loudly like brass trumpets, their snores in synchronization with each other.

If Metta had been awake, she would have laughed out loud.

Somewhere between dreaming and sleeping, Metta heard voices. They were all fuzzy at first, but gradually, the voices became clearer and louder. She opened one eye.

Mama was sitting up in bed. Her beautiful red hair with gray streaks in it lay in long tresses down her back. The moon reached down with its silvery beams and touched her face.

She was listening to someone.

"I can't help Daddy with the trapping. I just get in his way. He doesn't know what I can do, so he leaves me at people's houses so that he doesn't have to worry where I am. He didn't worry when Mother was still here."

Metta knew that voice.

It was Elsa.

"I get all broken up inside because I don't feel like I really belong to anybody." Elsa sniffled, rubbing her eyes with the back of her hand. "My heart is all sick, Mrs. McLaughlin. And I don't mean to keep you awake, you being sick and all, but I just had to know." A tear slid down her cheek. "If Jesus can heal you, can He heal me too?"

Mrs. McLaughlin's face was tender. "Yes, Elsa. He can do anything." She leaned forward and caught Elsa up in her arms and held her tight. Elsa cried in her arms. Mrs. McLaughlin smoothed Elsa's hair, put her mouth up to her ear, and whispered, "God loves you so much, Elsa." She wiped away Elsa's tears.

Metta swallowed the lump in her throat. She squeezed her eyes tightly shut.

And she prayed for Elsa.

It stopped raining sometime during the dark, early hours of the morning. But Metta wasn't awake to know about it.

She woke up, instead, to the smell of breakfast.

And to the sound of Heeter eating.

Heeter was sprawled out under the table, taking enormous bites out of a piece of corn bread. Little yellow crumbs were scattered all around him. He chewed noisily. "You know," Heeter said, "Claire makes corn bread a whole lot better than you do, Metta. Her corn bread tastes like what corn bread was meant to taste like. Yours tastes like a chunk of wood."

Metta threw back her blankets. "Where is Claire?" Almost everyone was up, but Claire was nowhere in sight. It was Naomi standing in front of the stove.

Since Heeter had his mouth full, his snicker came out in some sort of strange gurgle. "She's out taking care of the horses with Reed." He swallowed the last bit of corn bread and licked his fingers. "I tried to spy on them, but Reed found me and whipped my britches."

"You ought to have your britches whipped more often," Metta muttered, rising and grabbing up her blankets. She haphazardly folded them up and placed them in the corner. "Do you know where Elsa is?"

Heeter crawled out from under the table and snatched another piece of corn bread. He crammed it into his mouth. "Humpfa dabis gimmerinfis."

"Why don't you finish chewing first?" Metta crossed her arms, annoyed.

He gulped. "Why don't you wait until I'm done chewing before you ask me a question?" Heeter reached for a glass of milk. "Her dad's here to take her home."

Metta's eyes flew open, widening in astonishment. "What? Why didn't you tell me?" She raced out the door, barefoot, and her nightgown whipping against her legs.

Heeter called after her, "How was I supposed to know you wanted to say good-bye?"

Mr. Ramsey hoisted Elsa onto the back of his horse behind the saddle. He exchanged his thanks to Mr. McLaughlin, shoved his foot in the stirrup, and swung on up.

Metta skidded to a halt five feet away, breathless and grubby.

"You better write me!" Metta shouted. "We're the best of friends, remember?"

Elsa didn't look so prissy or arrogant anymore. She looked like someone had healed her broken heart, and as she rode away, her smile widened when she yelled, "I remember!"

"I don't know if the stagecoach can get through this mud," Old George stood out on the porch, rubbing his grizzly white beard and frowning upon all the puddles of muddy water. "It would sink down in this mud for sure, and we wouldn't be able to get it out till summer."

Metta wiggled her toes; the mud squished between her feet.

"Just stay around here for a day or two till it dries out," Noah offered. "Me or Reed can ride into town and tell them you got hold up here cause of the weather. I'm sure Dad won't mind."

Heeter flew through the door and shouted, "Reed won't mind either!" Heeter yelled out, running from one end of the porch to the other. "It looks like a lake out here! Metta, we should make the trading post into a riverboat. McLaughlin Riverboat Company. You could do all the work, and I'd be in charge." He looked at her strangely for a moment. "Metta, do you know that you're standing out in the middle of our yard in your nightgown?"

Frowning, Metta hitched up her gown above her ankles. The hem of the nightgown was dappled with mud. She sloshed through the yard and up to the porch.

Reed climbed up the porch steps, leather straps of a harness slung over his shoulder. Claire, her hair all combed and put up prettily, was right beside him. He squinted perplexingly. "Metta," he began slowly, scratching his head. "What are you still doing in your nightgown?"

"It's a long story," Metta said tightly. "I'm going in to change now."

Heeter shoved his thumbs in his suspenders. "By the way, Reed," His lips spread out in a grin. "You should try Claire's corn bread. She's a really good cook. If you don't marry her, I will. I'm in love with her corn bread."

Claire and Reed blushed at the same time.

Reed, his face flaming red, chased Heeter off the porch, and Metta ran into the house.

"Thank you so much for your hospitality." Mr. Plinkerton shook hands with Mr. McLaughlin. "Old George gave us the proper directions to the Charles Bunion Hotel, so we'll be heading off right away."

Mrs. Plinkerton gathered up her children in her arms, clucking and calling to them like a mother hen would do to her chicks. They snuggled under her arms and gathered around her skirt. Mr. Plinkerton put their knapsack on his shoulder, and just before they left, he offered some advice.

"It would be best if Creaky Joe didn't try to move around for a couple of days," Heinrich suggested. "Lord-willing, the wound won't get infected. Change the bandages regularly." He pulled his hat snuggly on his head and led his family to the door.

Creaky Joe pushed himself up by his elbows, licked his lips, and said, "Thank you, Mr. Plinkerton."

Mr. Plinkerton stooped down and little Stefan scrambled up on his back and hung his arms around his neck. When he stood upright, Mr. Plinkerton answered, "Give your thanks to God, son. He's the one who saved you, not me."

Metta shut the door when they left and turned around. She was surprised to see her father helping her mother stand. Metta could hardly believe it. Her mother hadn't stood up in weeks.

"Let me try it on my own, Joseph," Mrs. McLaughlin smiled, slowly stepping out of her husband's arms. "I think I can do it." She took a few shaky steps, like a baby who was learning to walk for the first time.

"Well, whistle me Dixie," Old George stared, removing his hat from his head. A tear slid down his craggy face, but his eyes shone. "Jesus healed you, Mrs. McLaughlin. He surely did."

Mrs. McLaughlin looked all around the room—her eyes shining like stars at her husband, Old George, Creaky Joe, Noah, Reed, and Claire. She paused at Metta, and her brow creased in concern. "Metta dear, why are you still in your nightgown?" she asked curiously.

Heeter yanked open the door, sticking his scrawny, freckled face inside. "Hey, Metta." His sly voice coaxed Metta to look his direction. He grinned like a cat and held up a very dirty green ribbon, dangling it high in the air. "Look what I found out in the mud."

"Give it back!" Metta shouted. She hauled up her skirt and started chasing after him.

Laughing, Heeter dashed across the yard, jumping from puddle to puddle. He waved the ribbon above his blond head like a green flag, his buckteeth sticking out in front of his wide grin.

Metta closed in on him, forgetting once again that she was still in her nightclothes. Her bare feet made funny little tracks in the soggy ground, splashing up water and mud all over her gown.

But she didn't care.

Not at the moment, anyway.

The sun came out, and the little golden sunbeams came down and danced on the puddles. A rainbow, bright with every color you could imagine, split the skies above them. A cool breeze had just begun to blow as Metta tackled Heeter and finally got back her green ribbon.

The McLaughlin Family

Old George   Claire   Creaky Joe

The Plinkerton Family

CPSIA information can be obtained at www.ICGtesting.com
Printed in the USA
BVOW06s1918121016

464867BV00010B/128/P